Outside

by Deirdre Gill

For Christopher!

Deirdre Gill

HOUGHTON MIFFLIN HARCOURT
Boston New York

The world is full of magic things,

patiently waiting

for our senses to grow sharper.

—W. B. Yeats

www.hmhco.com

The text of this book is set in Stempel Garamond.
The illustrations are oil on paper.

Library of Congress Cataloging-in-Publication Data

Gill, Deirdre, author, illustrator.
Outside / by Deirdre Gill.
pages cm
Summary: When his brother refuses to come outside, a child plays by himself in the snow and creates an imaginary world.
ISBN 978-0-547-91065-9
[1. Snow—Fiction. 2. Play—Fiction. 3. Imagination—Fiction.]
I. Title.
PZ7.G39857Ou 2014
[E]—dc23
2013039034

Manufactured in China
SCP 10 9 8 7 6 5 4 3 2 1

4500480611

For Jason

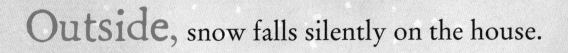

Outside, snow falls silently on the house.

Inside, a boy has nothing to do.

So he puts on his coat

and his boots,

wraps his scarf
around twice,

and steps outside.

PLOOOF!

He sinks into the soft snow–

and looks up.

"Come outside!" he calls to his brother.

But his brother won't.

So the boy begins to roll a
little clump of snow,

which gets bigger,

and bigger,

and when it will not roll
another inch,

he begins to build,

and play,

and build some
more, until

the castle is perfect.

That is when the dragon comes.

Together the boy and the
dragon fly over the trees,

over the house,

and above the village, until the world below
looks very small.

As the light begins to fade,
the boy knows that he must return to the forest

and go back inside,

but not before he and his brother

play outside.